THIS BOOK BELONGS TO

....

KALLIE GEORGE

SPLASH

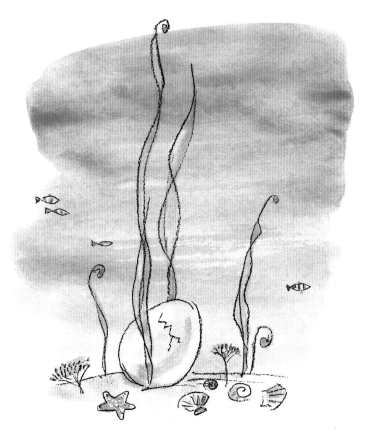

ILLUSTRATED BY

GENEVIÈVE CÔTÉ

SIMPLY READ BOOKS

To Jewell, who loves to splash. – K.G.

For my sisters Marie-Luce and Marie-Hélène, with love. –G.C.

Published in 2015 by Simply Read Books
www.simplyreadbooks.com
Text © 2015 Kallie George
Illustrations © 2015 Geneviève Côté

Library and Archives Canada Cataloguing in Publication
George, K. (Kallie), 1983–, author
Splash / written by Kallie George ;
illustrated by Genevieve Cote.

ISBN 978-1-927018-77-4 (bound)

I. Côté, Geneviève, 1964–, illustrator II. Title.

PS8563.E6257S65 2015   jc813´.6   C2015-902461-7

We gratefully acknowledge for their financial support of our publishing program the Canada Council for the Arts, the BC Arts Council, and the Government of Canada through the Canada Book Fund (CBF).

Manufactured in South Korea.

Book design by Naomi MacDougall.

10 9 8 7 6 5 4 3 2 1

CONTENTS

Surprise!

One day a tiny sea serpent was born.

She swam to the surface.

SPLASH! went her tail.

"Shush!" said Mama.

"Hush!" said Papa.

But her tail twitched and splished and SPLASHED.

"Splash!" cried the little sea serpent.

And that became her name.

Splash grew bigger.

Her tail did, too.

It made bigger and bigger splashes.

"Shush!" said Mama.
"Sea serpents are silent."

"Hush!" said Papa.
"Sea serpents are sneaky."

"But splashing is fun!" said Splash.

"Not if people hear and see you," said Papa. "You might get caught."

Splash tried to be quiet.

But every time, her tail twitched and splished and SPLASHED.

Mama and Papa went to Grampy for help.

Grampy was the most silent, sneaky sea serpent in the sea.

He was also the oldest and the wisest. He knew just what to do.

"It is time for Splash to have sea serpent swimming lessons," he said. "I will teach her myself."

Shadow Swimming

Splash followed Grampy to the surface.

"First I will teach you Shadow Swimming," said Grampy.

"YAY!" said Splash.

"Shh!" said Grampy. "Swim only in the shadows. Pretend you are a shadow. Do shadows splash?"

"No," said Splash.

"Right," said Grampy. "Time to hide. Follow me."

Grampy swam ahead. Soon he reached some shadows.

The shadows rippled. Grampy rippled, too. He looked just like a shadow.

Splash tried to ripple.

She tried to be like a shadow.

But her tail wouldn't let her. It twitched and splished and...

SPLASHED!

"Oops," said Splash.

Grampy frowned. "You'll have to practice your Shadow Swimming."

Log Floating

"Next I will teach you Log Floating," said Grampy. "Swim next to the logs. Pretend you are a log. Do logs splash?"

"No," said Splash.

"Right," said Grampy. "Time to hide. Follow me."

Grampy swam over to some
logs. He lay on his back. He
lay very straight and still.
He looked just like a log.

Splash lay on her back.
She stretched out straight.
She tried to be still.
She tried to be a log.

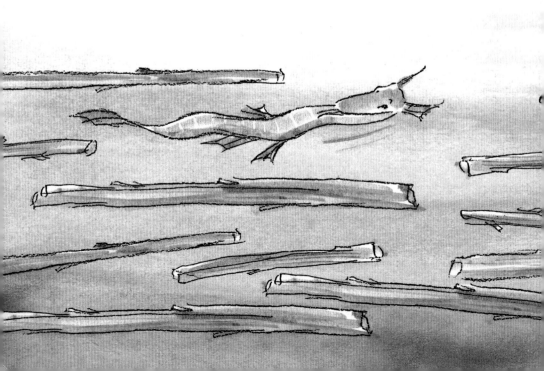

But her tail wouldn't let her.
It twitched and splished
and...

SPLASHED!

"Oops," said Splash.

Grampy groaned.
"You'll have to practice
your Log Floating."

Seaweed Sneaking

"This is the LAST lesson," said Grampy. "It is called Seaweed Sneaking. Dive down to the seaweed. Pretend you are a piece of seaweed. Does seaweed splash?"

"No," said Splash.

"Right," said Grampy. "Time to hide. Follow me."

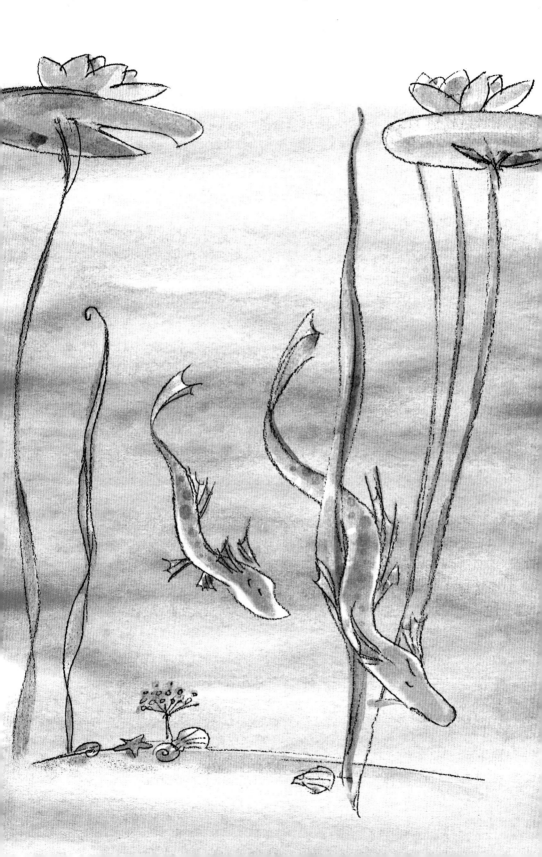

He swam over to some
seaweed. He dove deep.
Only his tail stuck up out
of the water.

The seaweed swayed.
Grampy's tail swayed, too.
It looked just like a piece
of seaweed.

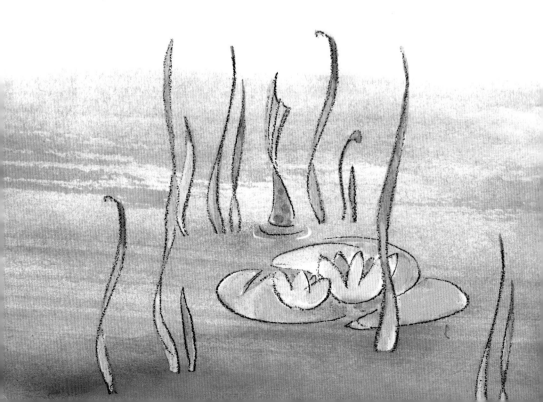

Splash dove deep. She stuck her tail out of the water.

She tried to be like a piece of seaweed. She tried extra hard.

But her tail wouldn't let her. It twitched and splished and...

SPLASHED!

"Oops!" said Splash.

Grampy sighed. "Let's try again tomorrow. It's time for supper."

"Okay," whispered Splash.

The Big Boat

Splash and Grampy started
swimming home.

They heard a noise.
Chug, chug, chug.

The noise grew louder
and louder.

"It's a boat!" said Grampy.
"Quick! Time to hide!"

There were no shadows or
logs or seaweed in sight.

Splash didn't know
what to do.

Grampy went still.

Splash went still, too.

She didn't try to be a shadow, or a log, or a piece of seaweed.

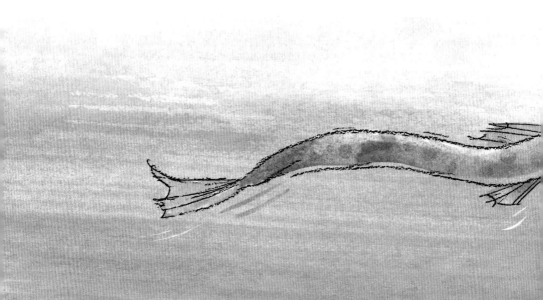

She was just herself.
But silent and sneaky.

And her tail let her!

It didn't twitch or splish or splash—not even a little!

Chug, chug, chug.

At last the boat left.

"Well done!" said Grampy.
He was proud.

Splash was prouder.

"I don't need to be a shadow,
or a log, or seaweed to be
still," explained Splash.
"I can be Splash without
any splashes."

"Yes, you can," said Grampy.

To celebrate, Grampy took Splash to a secret cave.

There she could be as loud and lively as she wanted.

But guess who made the loudest splashes of all?

THE END